LOST
IN THE
AMAZON

LOUANE K. BEYER

Library of Congress Control Number:		2013907517
ISBN:	Hardcover	978-1-4836-3122-6
	Softcover	978-1-4836-3121-9
	Ebook	978-1-4836-3123-3

This book was printed in the United States of America.

Rev. date: 04/30/2013

To order additional copies of this book, contact:
Xlibris Corporation
1-888-795-4274
www.Xlibris.com
Orders@Xlibris.com
132926

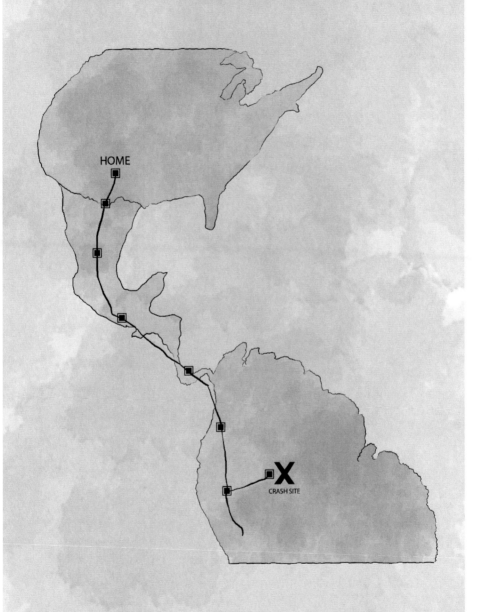

Contents

Illustrator:

Kenny Estrella

Along with Roger Beyer and grandchildren:
Emilee Lindseth
Adam Beyer
Abigail Beyer
Allie Beyer
Nathan Beyer

Acknowledgement

Thank you to my husband, Roger, who again has offered his expertise and knowledge attained during 26 years as a science teacher. A personal acknowledgement to Dr. Glen Johnson, an amateur "ham" radio operator, that is also a pilot of a single engine airplane. His experience in airplanes steered me in the right direction in choosing a plane that would be suitable for my story. Then to my granddaughter, Abby, who named it "Domitila" while taking Spanish lessons. It means "Cinderella".

Then to my family that has been most supportive in promoting our first book, offering ideas, and editing this book. For Allie, who made numerous appearances to sign and read. They all helped at book signing, expos and photo shoots.

Most of all though an appreciation for all the people who purchased my first book which in turn made this book a reality.

Dedication

To the scientists, environmentalists, school children, teachers and others who care to preserve the Rain Forests of the World.

There is great value to protect and maintain a rain forest like the Amazon Rain Forest for regulation of the global climate patterns. Rain forests are critical to the survival of the diversity of plants and animals. Located close to the equator for the abundant rainfall and sunshine needed on a continuous basis, the rain forests are able to thrive. They act as filters through the trees that absorb carbon dioxide and produce oxygen into the atmosphere.

As the author of "Lost in The Amazon", I did research reading manuals, periodicals and articles. It was a fascinating journey for me. One of the characters, the pilot Mannie, speaks of the loss of habitat, the history of the effects that the rubber industry had on the rain forest, and how the encroachment of civilization forever changed the way of life for the people and the natives who depend on the rain forest for a living. In the story, he maintains a compound that houses endangered species of the Amazon Rain Forest for specialists and environmentalists to study and preserve.

Their hope is to prevent extinction of many species. He speaks about the soil that is nutritionally poor and how the bountiful rainfall along with composted leaves allows the forest to survive.

My family and I share the optimism that you will learn much by reading our book about this exciting place on the face of the earth.

Chapter 1

SUMMER VACATION BEGINS

As the school buzzer sounded, the students rushed out of the building and tumbled into the school bus waiting at the curb. Peter, who was 13 looked at his 11-year-old brother, Andy, smiling said "Summer vacation is beginning." Sandy haired Andy grinned back commenting that it has been an awesome year. They both pulled out their report cards looking at them still amazed at the excellent marks they had received. They were silent for a few minutes listening to their younger sister, Abby, and cousin, Allie, chat about their July birthday parties. The youngest brother, Nate, was searching in his school bag for one of his favorite red Hot Wheel cars.

Finally, Peter said, "Andy, since school is out I think it would be a good idea for us to spend time together to speak about what happened last August. It seems as though when we got back there was so much excitement with school starting that it was like all put on a shelf." In response, Andy nodded his head and suggested that they go fishing in the creek tomorrow to reminisce.

Peter thought for a moment as memories of what had happened flashed through his mind. He could not believe that neither himself nor Andy ever once broached the subject of the nearly fatal trip all fall and winter.

Six days inside a mountain walking in search of food, water, and an exit to stay alive. Then add the encounter with the aliens, it seemed like a dream. It was not though. They both knew that something surreal had happened.

Peter finally agreed aloud that fishing would be just right. He added, "I'll bet mom and dad will watch us closely. Ever since we exited the mountain and there, miraculously, was dad, he doesn't let us get out of sight for long." Andy looked at Peter exchanging a glance. It was as if they could almost read each other's minds. Strange. As the bus came to a stop in front of their house, the five of them clamored out. They ran up the driveway knowing that their mom would have their favorite treat ready for them. It was a tradition to eat mini-tacos piled high with cheese. For once, mom did not caution them not to eat too much or they would not be hungry at supper. She gave them each a big hug as she watched them chatting and eating.

To everyone's surprise, their dad walked in the door. He called out, "I left work early today so I could get a share of the treats. Don't eat them all before I get a chance to wash up." The house rang with laughter and cheery giggles.

Later as they cleared out their book bags, each of them laid out their report cards on the counter, including Allie's even though they knew that her mom and dad would be inspecting hers later. Their dad picked up Peter's and Andy's cards, jerked in amazement as he looked them over.

He looked from Peter to Andy shaking his head quizzically said, "You both usually had fairly good grades but this year straight A's? I still can hardly believe what I am seeing here." Neither of the boys said anything knowing it was sort of news to them too. Andy said, "Dad, Peter and I thought we would go fishing in the creek tomorrow. We could go catch a few fish and clean them in time for supper."

Their dad stopped and looked at them almost in fear as he questioned them. He rubbed his forehead for a while reluctantly giving them permission. He looked at them with concern cautioning them to be careful and not to wander too far from home. He added, "Please take Buddy with you." They agreed then went out to the shed to get the poles, shovel, and a coffee can. While Peter turned over the soil to bring up the worms, Andy spoke about how worried dad was. Peter responded that he had noticed it also. He added, "You can bet on it that he will come by to check on us for sure." They finished getting the worms into the can adding some water to keep them moist.

As they entered the house, they both saw the worry on their parents' faces. Peter wondered what he could do to regain their trust in him.

Peter went to his room taking his school bag with him. He lay down on his bed and looked around his room. On the walls there hung large posters and pictures of outer space, airplanes, the moon, and space ships.

As he lay there, thoughts of last summer flooded back. He recalled how Andy and himself walked to the lowlands on the day after his thirteenth birthday eager to target practice with his new rifle. It was a hot day. They wandered around neither of them paying any attention as they climbed to higher elevations and, unknowingly, got lost. Because they had little food and water, they counted on their dad coming to their rescue as he knew the area well.

They gathered some boughs to make a lean-to and scraps of bark to build a fire that kept them warm and scared off any wild animals wandering by. While they both slept, sparks blew around as the wind came up starting the dry cinder and big trees on fire. Boxed in, they took refuge in a small, dark cave. Peter shook his head a bit remembering the guilt he felt thinking it was his fault. He was the oldest and his dad had trusted him. He remembered how they realized that rescue was out of the question. With limited supplies, their only solution was to walk deeper into the cave in search of water.

After sorting through their backpacks to see what they had, they decided to inch their way out of the cave to retrieve whatever they could despite the heat and wind. That was how their adventure began.

He remembered shooting the rabbit, gathering nuts and berries, the hundreds of flying bats, and the plan to walk into an unknown cave. He shivered recalling how ill he became, how he survived and then discovering the huge cavern with plentiful food and water. The encounter with the aliens and their spaceship lodged into the cave walls was incredible. It was a challenge but he was proud of how he and Andy devised a method to communicate with the aliens. The four of them helped each other to free themselves so the aliens could begin their journey back to their planet and themselves to go home. They walked out of the mountain never looking back, grateful to be well and safe as they met their dad. It was like a miracle had happened! Then Peter fell asleep. He heard a knock on his door with mom calling that supper was ready. He also heard a car in the driveway knowing that it was Allie's parents picking her up.

Chapter 2

DAD OFFERED ASSIGNMENT IN PERU

B ecause the children all slept in this morning, the parents along with Buddy, their pet dog, were extra quiet. It was overcast with some showers in the forecast. Brad assured his wife that the boys would stay close plus taking the dog with them added confidence. When they'd disappeared last August for six days, the family had prepared themselves for the worst. Now they didn't want to take any chances.

He would choke up remembering searching for days that seemed in vain. Then there they were right before his eyes! They told the story of getting lost, the fire, the cave, the search for food and water, then locating this opening on the other side of the mountain. He didn't ask many questions. While marveling at their survival, he wondered about what had really transpired. He knew that even today he would stop by the creek to see them.

Later that morning, Peter and Andy took their fishing poles, equipment, and worms to catch some fish. The hazy conditions were ideal for fish to bite. While Buddy stretched out on the grassy bank, the boys watched the bobbers hoping for a nibble. They laid down on the grass looking up into the sky. Peter pulled off a blade of green grass and began to chew on it. Oh, summer was great!

Finally, Andy said, "I wonder if our alien friends ever made it back to their planet. It was a long journey."

Peter answered that it was a relief that they were now talking about the aliens. He added, "Before they left, they looked into our eyes transferring some sort of energy to us. I could feel it as it flowed into my eyes giving strength to me. I can think more clearly. While math was so easy this year, I had to guard myself not to show my potential. It was like I was hiding a secret. What about you?" Andy agreeing said, "I also felt empowered with the gift. It is a burden not to talk about the space ship and the encounter with the aliens though. They were special to us. I have wondered though why they gave us the gift. Do you think that they could foresee into our future that we would have a special use for it?" He added that it confused him by what all this means.

Just then as their bobbers jerked, they jumped up to reel in the fish. It didn't take long to catch enough for a good meal. The boys headed home to clean them.

As they walked up the hill, they saw their dad's truck parked in the driveway. Peter laughing commented, "What did I tell you? I knew Dad would come to check on us." They put their gear on the back patio as the door slammed open and out rushed their parents both saying they had something to tell them. Andy asked if he was going to have a new brother or sister.

They all chuckled with mom saying no. Their dad began explaining, "I've been offered a contract from a national lumber company. It would entail travel to South America to investigate the probability of establishing a network to purchase lumber from the rainforest country near Iquitos, Peru. The company is interested in attaining rights to the lumber which is unique to that area. The project has been accepted but there are problems with the transportation. With no highways in or out of Iquitos, the only methods of transportation are airplanes or boats on the Amazon River and it's tributaries. They need someone with my expertise to develop a route which might include shipping it part way then trucking it or using the rail system north to America. It is an advantage that I speak fluent Spanish." He explained that the contract would mean much to us since the slowed economy has had an effect on house building. He added, "I know that I have the ability to see this to completion. Now for the best part, I would like to take you boys with me to South America. I figure the project will take about a week to set up. It is agreeable with your mom. We would leave in about two days so what do you say?" Peter and Andy jumped up at the same time to say that it would be exciting.

Andy asked, "Wow, Do you think we will be able to tour Machu Picchu, the Inca Empire? I read so much about it when we studied it in school." His dad shook his head saying, "No,

That is too far south in Peru and I will need to concentrate on Iquitos. I assure you though that I will try to take some time to tour some other areas close by." With this, Peter ran to the computer to 'google' the rain forest while Andy opened the encyclopedia as a source to look at. He used them often as the material was helpful. It was a set that his grandfather had purchased when their dad was a little boy and last year gave it to him.

Soon their dad called for them to clean the fish that he would cook after checking out some travel arrangements for them at the airport. They agreed reluctantly as they were immersed in searching for information while at the same time so excited with the adventure that lay ahead of them.

After Brad's return, he was elated as he shared some exciting news to the family. While cooking the fish, he told them that he had met a friend at the airport who introduced him to an independent pilot named Mannie.

He had just flown in with his Stinson 108-3 Flying Station Wagon from South America. The plane was an old one yet it looked to be well maintained. It was Mannie's pride and joy. He calls her 'The Domitila' that is 'Cinderella' in Spanish. The two of them discussed the project. Mannie agreed to fly them to Peru and back home.

They would leave day after tomorrow depending on what the weather conditions were along the route. "The plane," their dad explained "has a 2400 pound capacity with the empty weight at 1300 pounds. Then add in a full fuel load of 50 gallons, the passengers, baggage, and other cargo, Mannie figured the plane would do the job." He went on to describe that the plane was being powered by a reliable 165 Hp Franklin engine and conventional gear with two front wheels and a tail wheel necessary for bush landings. It is even bright red in color. He explained that he had been nervous about whether to use commercial air traffic or the alternate small plane. After looking at the plane and talking to the pilot, he believed it was a good choice to use the single engine airplane as it is more personal.

As they ate their meal, their dad said, "We have much to do and must prepare to pack carefully. I wonder how we will sleep tonight with all this." Abby and Nate added that they would like to go as well but then agreed that they would stay at home to help their mom.

As they went to their rooms, Peter and Andy decided they would start making a list of what they would need. They were certain that their parents would inspect what they were taking as there were weight restrictions as Dad had earlier described. Remembering the value of the extra supplies they learned from the experience last year, they knew they would stock their back packs with care.

Chapter 3

AIRLINE TRIP BEGINS

Just after dawn, the family met Mannie on the runway at the airport to prepare for takeoff. The bags were loaded and final checks were made.

Both Peter and Andy kept their back packs with them. Mom had tears in her eyes as she gave them each a big hug. She whispered for them to be safe and come back home. Next it was Abby, Nate, and Allie taking turns to say their farewells. They called out to be sure to write.

The passengers climbed aboard for the adventure ahead. Mannie revved the six cylinder Franklin engine, put on his headset to get clearance from the tower, and began to taxi down the runway. The plane shook and rattled with Mannie looking in the back seat chuckling saying to the passengers, "Sounds like this old rattle trap shakes until the rivets pop out. My girl here is old but you will see how she hums when we get airborne. Hoop! I got the signal to go. Hope you boys don't get air sick. I guarantee that you will feel light headed so pop your ears after we take off then you will be ok."

The plane started to rise, then banked off to the south when Mannie asked if they were alright. Peter and Andy did feel sort of sick yet neither would admit it. They looked at each other nodding an affirmative. Mannie liked to talk. His passengers listened with interest.

He explained that at sea level it takes about 600 feet for take off. We will take off at about 80 mph.

Most airports have long run ways which wasn't the case in many places that he flew. Sometimes it took some ingenuity to get airborne. He pointed to one of the instruments telling them he was climbing about 800 feet per minute until they would reach about 12,000 feet where he would level off with the cruise speed of about 121 mph.

Meanwhile, the three passengers looked out the windows studying the landscape below them where they saw the earth looking like a big patchwork with cleared land, tilled acres, forests, rivers, and many roads. Peter said that he was going to look for their school and house. Brad thought of his two sons who looked so brave. Peter was getting tall and gangly.

He participated in sports and Boy Scouts. More out spoken than quiet Andy, who was bookish and often shy, he let his feelings be known. He felt a twinge of regret as he knew he would liked to have spent more time with them and was now thankful that he had asked them to accompany him on this expedition. He smiled to himself as he wondered what they were thinking about their first airplane ride.

Mannie broke in and asked them if they knew much about aviation. The boys shook their heads to say no. Mannie began to describe that the Stinson has a fabric covered steel tube with a tall vertical fin with the rudder featuring a straight trailing edge.

It helped to make the plane more efficient when the company updated the plane's fuel capacity. He went on to say, "We will travel about 118 mph for the next four hours then we will land to fuel up. The airports that I have chosen on my flight path are on a safe route to avoid travel warnings about violence perpetrated by the drug cartels and bandits."

Peter and Andy plugged in their Ipods and listened to music while their dad called their mom on his Iphone. As predicted, the airplane hummed as they kept an eye on the scenery below.

Soon Mannie got the boys' attention by describing the cockpit and instrument panel. He said, "Lean forward and see them as I point out what each one does. First here is the compass which shows direction of travel by the use of a magnetic needle. It swings free on a pivot pointing to the 'magnetic north'. Over here is the fuel gauge which measures how much fuel there is in the supply tank. Along side here is the oil pressure and temperature gauge which would be critical if there was a slow leak. It would unravel the engine due to heating up."

He went on to point out the tachometer. Most all vehicles have them and I'll bet your dad has one on his truck that you have seen him check often. The ammeter is an instrument measuring the strength of electric current in amperes. Mannie then went on pointing to the air speed indicator saying, "This tells me how fast I am going in knots or mph. I

am sure you both understand what mph is but how do you convert it to knots? A knot is a unit of speed equal to one nautical mile which is approximately 1.151 mph. So if I am traveling 143 mph, what would that be in knots? Andy and Peter looked at each other. Almost simultaneously they said, "124 knots." "Whoa," Mannie choked as he looked over at Brad who just shrugged and smiled. "You two surprised me," he said, "We are traveling at 121 mph which would be 105 knots." He went on then to describe the altimeter that shows the aircraft's height above sea level. Here is the attitude indicator that shows me how the plane is in relation to the horizon. It will show me if the wings are level or if my airplane's nose is pointing above or below the horizon. This may be a lot to remember but we will be landing and taking off often then it will be more understandable.

Mannie then directed his attention to the airport they were approaching and talked with the tower for directions. They landed softly feeling hardly anything thinking that Mannie is a good pilot. They thanked him for all the instrument descriptions. They got out of the plane and walked about while it was refueling. It didn't take long before they were back in the air humming along. The boys were tired. They laid back their seats and fell asleep for several hours rocking in the plane which performed like a well tuned machine. Soon their dad called for them to wake up as it was time for another landing for a fuel and a pit stop. As Mannie was approaching the building, he became alarmed saying, "Something is not right here. I hope I am wrong but you three stay put in the plane. Let me handle this."

Sure enough as Mannie opened his door to get out, there were men aiming guns right at the airplane. They ordered all the passengers to deplane. The boys strapped their back packs on and climbed out of the seats. Their dad's face turned white with a frightened look. What Mannie had talked about was now a reality.

Chapter 4

TAKEN HOSTAGE

The group of bandits pushed and shoved them into the hangar with force. They were seedy looking, unkept and smelled of body odor. In addition, their language was hard to understand and sounded vulgar. They motioned for each of the captives to sit and bound them with ropes on their hands and feet. Duct tape was slapped across their mouths.

Mannie was an exception with the three of them watching in horror as they began to interrogate him. They shoved a rifle into his backside. It was a big one that looked much like an AK 7.62. Several of them had large pistol holsters attached to their belts. One of them brought out his pistol hitting Mannie across the side of his head with such force it drew blood. Mannie's eyes narrowed with a look becoming hard and cold like steel. They kept asking Mannie over and over again where he came from and where he was going. Mannie just answered that he was an independent pilot and was transporting a businessman and his children to Peru.

This went on relentlessly for hours. Mannie did not change his story. Then they asked for guns and money. When Mannie didn't answer, they hit him again. This time he hung his head and stayed that way for quite awhile. The bandits said they were holding the regular staff captive in another part of the building.

One of them had a cell phone and was making calls to report what was going on.

He nodded as if to say yes to the person on the other end. He mumbled something to the leader doing the interrogation of Mannie saying he wanted the bundle of money that Mannie was carrying. They said they had searched the airplane and couldn't locate anything except the cargo of batteries and supplies that was worthless to them.

Mannie shook his head telling them again that he had no money bundles and their information was incorrect. The interrogator finally said to him, "Do you know who we are?" To which Mannie shook his head that he didn't know. The guy said back, "Don't you watch television? We belong to a cartel with informants in the government. We can do what we want with you and your bunch here. No one can do anything about it?" One of the other guys snickered in the background.

The boys' dad was silent and worried that they would start on him and his sons soon as they weren't getting anything they wanted out of the pilot. He looked at Mannie who had blood stains on his shirt. Brad feared they would do the same or worse to himself. He would not take it if they began to torture Peter and Andy. He could only imagine what else could happen.

Mannie's head dropped to one side and he closed his eyes. He tried to co-operate but was only making it worse. In all of his years as a pilot and the different places he had been, he was thinking this stink hole was about the worst place. He knew that worse stuff would happen soon.

The interrogator snootily said, "You will give us the information we ask within the next hour then you know what is going to happen. Your government will be of no assistance to you and these other people here. Our informants tell us that your government sends aid to our government to break us up but that is of no use to our war that we are waging here."

Mannie stammered back that he had no information to give or what it was they wanted to know. He kept repeating this, "I have no bundles of money or guns. We are on our way to South America and meant no harm to any one here. I beg of you to let us go. We will not say anything to anyone." The interrogator looked at him with a hard stare then spit on him.

The bandits all left the room. They could hear them arguing about what they should do next and who to start with. Mannie swallowed hard saying, "I should have been more careful in landing here but I have used this airport many times. The people working here were honest and seemed friendly. I never would have imagined this would happen. We will be lucky to get out of this alive and even if we do, I wonder what they did to my 'Domitila'. She is all that I have to earn a living with." He hung his head in shame. They could hear that the bandits were talking on the phone again with their voices getting loud as they argued amongst themselves.

As they entered the room, they appeared to be agitated with each other as two of them came to Peter and Andy. They grabbed the back packs and began to rummage through them looking at what was in them. Peter and Andy looked at each other then nodded their heads in affirmation. As the two bandits looked up at them, the boys stared into each of the bandit's eyes. They stopped all activity as if they were mesmerized. The boys' eyes held them for several minutes.

A strange thing happened. The two bandits slowly began to put the articles back into the packs and returned them to the boys. They took off the duct tape and cut the ropes. Next they moved to Brad doing the same to him. The interrogator and another bandit stared in disbelief at what was happening. They whispered in their ears and left the room.

Mannie also looked on in disbelief and asked, "What just happened here? What did you two boys do to them?" Peter answered, "We just looked at them." Their dad was stunned as well.

The bandits came back into the room with a different manner telling them that they were free to go. They could refresh themselves, fuel the airplane and take off. Brad helped Mannie get up to go to clean off the blood and tend to his wound. Mannie said that he was ok and that they should leave quickly. Without delay that is exactly what happened. In short order, they were airborne again. Peter and Andy looked back and saw a jeep-like vehicle drive out of a hanger. There were several bandits with what looked like heavy artillary ready to aim at them but by then the plane was too high in the sky.

Andy quietly whispered to Peter, "That was so scary. I've seen stuff like that on television never dreaming that this could happen to us. Did you see how frightened Dad was?" Peter put his finger to his lips motioning not to say anything more right now.

Chapter 5

REPORT OF STALLED YACHT IN PACIFIC

They were all quiet as they looked out the windows at the scenery below. Finally Peter started the conversation asking Mannie about the mountains below. Mannie who seemed to be getting his pep and energy back answered, "This country is so beautiful. Look at the way the mountain range looks like a big V at the bottom with the west extension running north along the Pacific Coast and the east one along the Gulf of Mexico. We are flying over the volcanic region." Andy commented as he looked out his window that the clouds looked like big, puffy pieces of cotton. The sunshine was so bright and clear with excellent visibility. Peter said, "Last year, we were at a 'ham' radio operator's house for Boy Scouts Jamboree on the Air. The operator, NOFBA, told us that during the earthquake that hit in this area many years ago, he helped relay messages from the local operators in the area to people who were searching for relatives and friends. It was most interesting."

He added that the transceiver radio equipment hams use are sometimes the only link to the rest of the world until telephone and other types of communication can be restored.

Mannie really perked up as he said, "The radio I have here in the dash is a two way with all sorts of frequencies on it in addition to monitoring a steady hum that tells me that I am on course. I don't know if you noticed but there is a wire strung across the top of the plane that is the antenna.

The radio is a short wave Hallicrafter. It isn't often that I have any company on the many trips I take. My 'Domitila' here doesn't answer back so I decided to learn about Citizen Band but that was too limited. That led me into amateur radio. I haven't reached the highest class which is the extra but I am doing well as a general class. I so enjoy the hobby. Though ham radio operation requires an FCC license to use different frequencies, in case of emergency any frequency can be used. Some days I just monitor my Icom 706 to listen to what the locals are talking about and sometimes I break in as they like to hear from outsiders as well. How much do either of you know about ham radio and morse code?" Andy spoke up first saying," We practiced it for awhile so we know some about it."

"Yeah," chimed in Peter. Their dad also said he knew about Cbers but not much about amateur radio. He was amazed at what his sons knew.

He turned to the boys saying, "A trip like this is just what we needed to get to know more about each other. I am usually so busy with work, chores, and hunting that we lose track of important things"

Brad looked over at Mannie and asked if he thought that the bandits at the last pit stop should be reported. Mannie was silent for awhile then said to leave it to him to report. He told the three of them that his head ached some but a few aspirin were helping that. He thanked Brad for helping to clean his wound. Brad looked back at Peter and Andy saying, "I was frightened for what could have happened. I am proud of how you both acted showing strength of character. Still it is strange that they suddenly released us. If I had any inkling of danger such as that, I would not have put you two in harm's way and risk your lives. I love you both." He smiled at them but Peter and Andy noticed a tear in his eyes. They looked at each other and almost choked, wishing they could tell him the rest of the story. Peter though mused that he believed his dad's trust in him was restored.

The boys' dad asked about eating as he was getting hungry and looked back at his sons who nodded that they were also starved. Mannie said it was not too far until the next stop giving them some time to get out, move around and order some food. They waited for him to check the fuel and oil. Together they walked into the airport for some excellent tacos and enchiladas. The aroma greeting them gave them assurance that this was a good place to eat leaving them with a good memory of it.

It was a large airport with lots of activity so no one worried about repeating what had happened at the last stop. Just as Mannie had promised, the food was so tasty with the four of them taking their time to fill up, even ordering a dessert. Peter and Andy stopped off at the gift shop to pick up some post cards to sign and mail off to Abby, Allie, and Nate. They found some interesting maps and brochures tucking them into their back packs to read later on. Their dad located them and decided he would purchase a card as well to send to their mom. Mannie stayed in the food area having another cup of coffee while the three of them were in the gift shop. They spoke some about the different kinds of magazines and books there were here compared to what they had in the gift shops at home. They took some time to fill out the cards and thought of some interesting comments to write on them. They laughed when they thought of how excited the family would be to receive the cards in the mail. The attendant helped them with the right amount of postage and offered to put them in the mail slot to be picked up and ready to go out the next day.

They were so full from the big meal they had just eaten that it was a relief to walk around and get some exercise. They went back to find that Mannie was still sitting by the café table reading the current newspaper.

He smiled as they returned and filled them in on what was happening to the rest of the world according to the paper and what the comics page had to bring some humor to the reader's life.

It was getting dark and Mannie suggested they get some rooms at a hotel next to the airport to get some rest. He

was bushed. If he was flying by himself he thought he would have gone on. He knew the family had an eventful day and needed some sleep. Some pillow time would help him recuperate as well

They took an airport limo to the hotel to check in with Brad and the boys taking a room with double beds. Mannie checked into a single. He suggested they get a wake up call for 4:30 in the morning giving them a good start on the day to keep on schedule. With that, he hit the sack falling into a deep sleep.

He awakened several times with nightmares of what had occurred and what might have even been worse. A thought crossed his mind though still wondering what the boys did to the bandits to have them change their actions but for now he let it be. He would have more opportunities to ask on another day.

They met as scheduled, ate a hearty breakfast, got some items for lunch plus juices and coffee. They headed to the tarmac to continue the journey to Iquitos, Peru.

The sun was just peeking over the horizon spreading its rays that gave them all an exhilarating view of the landscape along with the canopy of trees and rivers. It was going to be a beautiful day ahead. They chatted some as they were rested and optimistic about the trip ahead. The airplane was running smoothly making it possible to visit in spite of the sound it made.

The boys put on their headsets to listen to their Ipods. Mannie and Brad visited about accommodations in Iquitos. Brad asked how safe would the boys be to leave them at the hotel where he had made their reservations.

Mannie thought for awhile saying, "Brad, I have an excellent suggestion.

It would be an honor to have you and the boys stay at my hacienda. It is close to the airport and I have plenty of room. My staff is Raol, who tends to the buildings. Cama, my housekeeper, is about the best Mama Mia anyone could ask for." Brad said that he wouldn't want to take advantage but that would be a great relief to him. "You know my meetings are not too far from the airport so I would be close to them as well," he added. Mannie shook his head indicating it was settled then. He went on adding that the boys would have a great time as he had a compound with a variety of birds and animals in enclosures including a playful monkey that often roamed about the house. They chuckled as they wondered how their young passengers would react to the good news. Mannie said that he would contact Raol to make arrangements.

Today was such a pleasure for all of them as they had plenty of food and juices to drink. They chatted some about how calm the Pacific Ocean was. It seemed endless. Andy looked down and said, "Dad, look out your window at the big ship way out there. It looks to be in trouble." Brad agreed and alerted Mannie to what they were witnessing.

It was a big luxury yacht probably from one of the area resorts loaded with passengers waving shirts and towels hoping to attract the attention of an aircraft. Mannie searched records to see if he could find what frequency he could contact them but could not. He told his passengers that he would use his Hallicrafter to call the Coast Guard.

He called for a control tower to give his location in longitude and latitude telling them he had a visual of the yacht that looked to have lost power and was drifting. The Control Tower took over the situation advising Mannie that they would have a search and rescue set up.

This added a lot of excitement for the plane's passengers. Mannie dipped the plane's wings some to let the yacht know that they were going to get some assistance. He asked Peter and Andy if they were interested in how airplanes and ships navigate? Andy answered for both of them, "We did wonder how the Coast Guard would find them with the numbers you gave them."

Mannie began by explaining that for centuries, people thought the earth was flat. Expeditioners, like Columbus, were sent out to look for new shipping routes. Devices were invented to aid the sailors. The first man to sail around the world was Magellan who proved that the earth was round.

In order for sailors to measure distance, they needed a method to start counting from the same place. A number of lines called meridians were drawn from the north and south poles. The prime meridian being at Greenwich, England. These imaginary lines can measure distance from lines of longitude and latitude in degrees. Of course today we use radar and radios." Brad was the first to speak relating on how he knew of them but this was the best explanation and turned to look at Peter and Andy who shook their heads in agreement. Peter said, "When I go to the library next time, I know that I will study the globe closely."

It was time for a fuel and stretch stop. The boys were excited to get airborne after picking up some snacks. They were careful to choose items that would not leave crumbs in the airplane. They did not spend much time on the tarmac as the next great wonder they would see is the Panama Canal Zone. They checked the maps and information they had picked up in the gift shop taking time to study more about the Panama Canal Zone, especially Andy who liked this sort of research. The sense of adventure had returned to the passengers of the 'Domitila.'

Not only Peter and Andy but also their dad were anxious to get an aerial view of the Panama Canal. They had heard so much about it. There was excitement as Mannie detoured from the planned route to allow the three of them to see the zone. Andy shared that he had read a book about Panama and related some of what he remembered. Andy told them that the canal crosses the Isthmus of Panama that is a long, narrow strip located between North and South America.

For many years, it was a dream of many businessmen to join the Pacific and Atlantic Oceans. Up to that point, ships had to travel around the tip of South America. Then in the 1900s, the United States built the canal with the help of thousands of laborers cutting through the jungles and swamps fighting mosquitoes, malaria, yellow fever, and even the bubonic plague carried by rats.

Then Peter remembered a series on the History Channel about it. He said, "Dad, we all watched it after Grandpa told us about it." Their dad then recalled how the locks were built to raise and lower ships. He told them about the chambers with huge steel gates. Then through the use of valves, the ships are raised to the level of the lake. It was a fascinating documentary. He looked at Andy and Peter thanking them for recalling this important piece of history.

They were able to look down at the canal zone amazed to see the number of ships that were transported through there. Even Mannie was silent as they watched the operation below them. They could see the massive construction in progress in expanding the locks. Brad asked them to look at the different flags on the ships showing the variation of ships that moved through there. He also commented on viewing the difference of the Atlantic to the Pacific Ocean. Mannie offered that the Pacific Ocean is larger and deeper than the Atlantic. Also the earth's crust is weak with frequent earthquakes and has thousands of volcanoes.

Now, the Atlantic Ocean has a S-shaped ridge running along the entire bed. Also our great Amazon River gushes fresh water into it. I heard that NASA has a satellite that was launched aboard an Argentine space craft a year or so ago to study salt content on the ocean surface waters. Both Peter and Andy were closely listening to the conversation as their dad told something that his dad had spoke of when he was aboard a submarine during a tour. He said it was a region called Sargasso Sea in the North Atlantic bounded on the west by the Gulf Stream, on the east by the Canary current, and the south by the Equatorial current. The system of ocean currents form the North Atlantic Gyre that deposit marine plants and refuse they carry out to the sea. The Sargasso Sea is known for the deep blue color and exceptional clarity with underwater visibility. The submarine captain was so impressed with this that he called for all engines to stop and drift in order for the crew to examine it. Brad turned and told his sons that Grandpa took a grappling hook to grab up the seaweed which was full of small organisms. The boys and Mannie were amazed to hear this. Mannie stated that they had to turn westward to follow the flight plan with them looking back to appreciate the view and the work that was done to make such a marvel possible and remember the Sargasso Sea.

Chapter 6

ON TO CALI

Mannie studied his maps coming up with the suggestion that they continue flying on to Cali where he had some friends who they could bunk with. He assured Brad that they would be safe as it is a friendly, hospitable home. "In America," he said, "you might call it a bed and breakfast. I sort of feel that I need a break and could use some shut eye."

Brad shook his head telling him that he trusted his judgment. They would be willing to accept the invitation asking Mannie if the friends knew that they would be coming. Mannie said, "I often just pop in on them but I will give them a call to see if they have room for the four of us."

He picked up his cell dialing their number and after talking a few minutes, he shook his head affirmatively. Mannie then said the last leg of the flight to Iquitos in the morning would be short. It would be better as they would arrive earlier in the day giving them the opportunity to get to his hacienda. They talked in quiet tones between the two of them as they did not want to let on about the surprise they had planned for the two young passengers.

Brad was pleasantly surprised as they arrived at the ranch as it had a private landing strip. A jeep was waiting to take them to the ranch. The driver was so pleasant giving them a short tour describing that their main crop here was coffee. With the moderate climate that varied little during the year, it was ideal for the coffee bean plant. The soil was rich with plants growing well with the plentiful rainfall. This being June, it was almost the end of the rainy season with trees, lawns and flowers in full bloom.

After meeting the owners, Brad spoke of the beautiful location with the foothills, coastal, and mountainous areas. He also thanked them for their generosity in offering them accommodations in this amazing, spacious ranchero. He introduced his two sons with great pride.

The evening was filled with food, music and good company. Later Peter said to Andy, "I felt the same about us finding this place as when we found the cavern in the mountain last August. It is almost like a dream to be here with these people who are so kind and generous."

Andy added that he liked the stables. He could imagine what it would be like to ride horses along the ocean with the waves lapping at their hooves. They turned in and slept so well in this safe, quiet, and beautiful place. Neither heard their dad come to the room to get some sleep also.

After a quick breakfast, it was off to the landing strip to head towards their destination, Iquitos. They would also get to see their first glimpse of the Amazon River and rain forest jungle.

Mannie checked in with the control tower getting confirmation on his route to Peru. After they were airborne, Mannie was his old self today. He began to tell the story of where the Amazon began high in the Andes Mountains in a small stream gaining momentum as small streams drained into it. The Amazon River consists of an extensive number of major river systems from several South American countries as it leaves the Andean terrain. It is surrounded by flood plains. Many times the forested banks are just out of the water as the river reaches flood stage as it reaches the enormous Amazon Rain Forest.

As Mannie directed the plane in a southerly direction, he was the usual talkative guide that the passengers were used to by now. He shared more information about the Amazon River. He said, "It is the largest river in the world beginning at a remote site where a small wooden cross sits just a short distance from the Pacific Ocean over 18,000 feet in the Andes Mountains. How humble is that? The Amazon was named after battling warrior women similar to the Amazons of Greek mythology."

He explained that the snow capped peak called Nevado Mismi is a glacial stream flowing from west to east to Iquitos where I live. Then it gathers steam. This makes it tremendously fast flowing through heavily forested area which has the most extensive habitat in the world.

Mannie asked them to recall what the latitude was as the Amazon River gathers water from 5 degrees north latitude to 20 degrees south latitude from an inter-Andean plateau that is a short distance from the Pacific Ocean. He went on to describe that in some places the river can be as much as 30 miles wide. The river winds eastward over a thousand miles ending up in the Atlantic Ocean on the other side of South America. The rainy season which extends from November through June is the reason for this. The tributaries do not flood at the same time but they do begin to recede in June. At places, the Amazon is comprised of multiple channels which connect to a complicated system of natural canals that cut through low, flat islands.

Mannie's passengers were silent as they listened in amazement. He continued to tell them that he loves this country and has flown many a mission along the river. "I chose Iquitos as my home and couldn't think of ever leaving it. Soon you will see all this for yourselves."

He went on to say more about his favorite place in the world. "Iquitos is a unique place in Peru. It is the largest city in the Amazon Rain Forest serving as a major port. Get ready for this number. We get about 103 inches of rain every year making for a hot, humid climate. There are no major highways so we use the river and airplanes. The logging industry is huge in this area. No basic food crop has been found that will grow here. I talk and talk, don't I?" he said.

He looked over at Brad and nodded his head indicating that this would be a good time to tell them what they had decided about lodging. Brad turned to the boys saying, "Mannie has asked us to stay at his place. He has not taken on any flying jobs this week to accommodate our stay here.

He lives close to the airport which is close to where I will be holding my meetings. It sounds like he has an interesting home with some unusual pets! Mannie has offered to take you both on some tours. What do you say?" The boys were wide eyed and excited that they would have this chance. They both knew they would learn a whole lot this week for sure. Brad then called the airport hotel to cancel their reservation.

Mannie spoke up saying, "There is one more piece of history about the Amazon Basin that I can share with you. A milky latex oozes from the bark of the wild rubber tree. Native Indians water proofed jars by pouring it over a mud mold then smoking it over a fire. They broke the mold extracting the pieces. My relatives told me that explorers from foreign countries brought the news to the rest of the world which began a long string of experiments for years. Finally someone added sulphur to it to make it pliable. From that, the tire was developed which began the boom lasting for at least 25 years. Tappers were used to locate the trees, collect the latex, smoke it then carried it back to places like Iquitos. It was a tragic time for our country. Camps sprung up with the madness to get the latex through the use of cheap labor including the local Indians. Many atrocities occurred, even slavery was used. It finally ended when the beans from the trees were grown in other countries and a cheaper method was devised." The boys listened quietly taking in what he said.

Mannie checked his instruments than said, "Oh, look there is the first sight of the Iquitos airport. I need to check in with the control tower to land on a side runway closer to those buildings over there. My 'Domitila' sits in a nice hangar when she is parked here. Raol will be waiting for us there."

Chapter 7

MANNIE'S HACIENDA

Just as Mannie told them about Raol, he appeared offering to help with the bags. The vehicle he drove was a strange looking contraption that looked like some different ones welded together. There was a cage on the back, a small open area, and seats that were enclosed like a jeep. Raol looked much like Mannie except when he smiled many of his teeth were missing. Peter and Andy liked him immediately.

Mannie told them that besides airplane matters, he also had some cargo to take care of. After greeting Raol, Brad called for a vehicle to take him to the office building. Before he left though, he hugged his two sons chiding them to listen to instructions and stay close to the house. Peter said, "Dad, we will be well taken care of by Raol. See you later on." Both boys waved to their dad as they climbed into the jeep. With that Raol pulled off the tarmac and headed in another direction talking the whole time. He was excited to have company this week, especially these two youngsters. They listened with great attention to the varied stories he had to tell.

It did not take long before they arrived at Mannie's place. As they stepped out of the jeep, they were amazed at what they saw. It was not just a house but a sort of compound with a hacienda, including side buildings. There were cages filled with all sorts of birds and animals making a huge cacophony of chirping, screeching, cawing, growling, snarling, and more. Raol told them not to mind the commotion as the birds and animals were not used to company.

The house was built with adobe colored bricks and a red tiled roof.

It was a long, low building with both a front and side entrance. Raol opened the front side as they entered.

Peter and Andy looked around a room they could not have imagined existed. Many of the walls had wool carpets or rugs in deep, rich colors hanging on them. Andy said, "Peter, I am amazed at the colors here which go from bright red to orange. Then look at the yellow which could have come from a dandelion in the sunshine." Peter agreed adding that he liked the dark green and the royal blue that looked soft to touch. Others had designs of animals, plants, and even beautiful, geometric designs. One whole wall was rock that gave the room a feeling of strength. Then there was a huge aquarium with water so clear it was nearly impossible to see it. It had some of the most colorful fish anyone could imagine. The boys were speechless and looked around in awe of the surroundings.

Cama entered the room welcoming the boys. She was a short, stocky woman with a warm, friendly voice saying to Peter and Andy, "You two must be famished! Follow me to the kitchen while Raol takes your bags to the room down the hall." They realized how hungry they were. The food looked so good and without ado, dug right in eating rice, corn, and beans that had a spicy, zesty flavor.

Cama told them that this dish is a favorite of the Peruvians as the herb, Ocas, adds much flavor. She said that she loves to cook and would fix them big meals. As they ate, Cama kept up a conversation with them about the house, the animals, Raol, and Mannie. She spoke in a broken Spanish/English with both of them understanding most of what she said. She told them that Raol liked to tell stories of the olden days. They would learn much from him while they were staying here.

By this time, Raol went back to pick up Mannie who had completed his tasks. He joined in the conversation telling Cama and Raol about the adventures they had experienced on the way here. "By the way" Mannie said, "I checked up on that yacht that appeared to be dead in the water. It was towed into the resort with some angry passengers as they had lost power. The passengers were not able to shower and the food was limited as there was no power to cook anything. They even complained that their cell phones did not work. They were safe now though." He added that more than likely the cruise line would give them compensation or some free ticket to use later on. We helped them out. Andy thanked Mannie for the news. They adjourned back to the living room where Mannie kept up a stream of informational talk. He took them to the aquarium to tell them about the fish he had stocked in there. He explained that he is often gone so he has a local pet store maintain it for him. The pet store keeps a variety of tropical fish and changes them out often. Andy and Peter peered into the aquarium to see the odd shapes, sizes, and colors. Just like the carpets on the wall, the tropical fish were bright yellow, orange, black, striped, and had a variety of spots and stripes. It was a marvel to them as they had strange markings and moved differently in the water.

Mannie went on to add that to the best of what he has heard there are more than 5000 types of neo-tropical fishes in the Amazon. He said, "I know for sure that Iquitos is a major supplier of tropical fish to the world nations. There is an airline dedicated for the purpose of shipping and transporting them. I have another aquarium in the study that has piranha in it. There are some 30 to 60 species of piranhas. Known as carnivorous fish, they gather into large schools and have a reputation of attacking their prey. The Red Bellied Piranha is the only species known to attack people. Later on I will show you the aquarium. For now, I would like to take a rest." He added that dinner would be late as they planned to wait for Brad. The boys could walk around but stay close by. He also told them that he had talked to their dad who was already in meetings about the lumber contract.

As Peter and Andy walked back to their room, they felt a real connection with Mannie. They expressed to each other the privilege of being with him. Several hours later, their dad walked into their room announcing that dinner was ready. He escorted them to the main dining room. Cama served them steamed shrimp fixed in a red colored sauce served on fluffy rice. There were so many delicacies that Peter and Andy selected several with each having its own particular flavor.

While they ate, music came from speakers mounted around the room

It sounded like a rich, deep percussion that could be heard but did not interfere with conversation.

Mannie asked Brad how the session went today. Brad responded with a comment, "I am satisfied so far. It is fortunate that I know how to speak Spanish and by the way thanks for offering to give any assistance that I need."

Mannie began a story about the Spaniard explorers who arrived somewhere during the 16th century. They had a great influence on the culture of the country of Peru. There were Indian tribes who developed a highly civilized empire known as the Incas over 700 years before then. The Land of Incas is located on the west coast high in the heart of the Andes Mountains.

They were advanced in astronomy, medicine, architecture, accounting, and social structure. Even today there is evidence of what they had developed at Machu Picchu. Much of the place is shrouded in mystery.

"From what I have read," Mannie said, "the Spaniards attacked the Incas capturing the emperor. For the next three hundred years, Peru remained under the rule of the Spanish."

"Wow!" exclaimed Andy, "When dad told us about coming to Peru, I was excited to see the place the Incas lived. In school, we studied some about the place. I know that it is too far south to go to see this trip. It is interesting to hear about. Someday I may visit the site." His dad shook his head saying, "I am satisfied that you understand that the business trip takes priority." Mannie smiled as he looked at his three guests inviting them to the library room as he had some things to show them.

They followed Mannie down the hall wondering what sort of surprise he had. As they entered the room, there was a big screech. The boys became enthralled with the sight of a huge toucan perched on a branch extending from a cage. Mannie went to the bird talking in a quiet tone.

Then there was more commotion as the guests turned to look at one more cage that held a little monkey. Mannie said, "Let me introduce you to my little friend, Zoey." He opened the cage and the monkey climbed on his shoulder. He motioned for the boys to slowly approach. She was so cute. The boys both marveled as they watched her. She had rather long, reddish colored hair covering the back of her head and most of her body. Her big,

brown eyes were riveting and her small tongue stuck out a bit from her mouth. Her hands and feet were like long fingers that they supposed she used to wrap around branches. Her manner was curious as she studied them. Peter slowly walked over to the monkey followed by Andy. They clucked their tongues a bit. The monkey began to chatter. Mannie reached up and petted the monkey who jumped on Andy's shoulder. Andy said, "Our grandfather was a science teacher. He told us stories of the animals that he had in his class room. One story was about a monkey that the students were thrilled with. They learned about care, feeding, and cleaning. The monkey liked to climb up to the fluorescent bulbs and sit to watch what was going on. One day our grandfather took the monkey to his mom's place for awhile. It got loose, climbed up a telephone pole, and ran outside along the lines. It was humorous for the towns people to see a monkey running on the wires until it was captured."

Mannie just laughed when he heard the story. He put the monkey back into its cage for the night. Then he explained that he didn't have any televisions in his house. He kept busy with the aquariums and the animals outside. Before turning in, he gave the boys a game to play he called 'Mexican Train' explaining it was a domino game that the boys would find challenging. He explained that the game is played with numbered dominoes off one another. "The chunky dominoes are clearly marked with numbers rather than dots which makes it easier to see, count and tally scores at the end of each round," he added. Peter and Andy played the game until late in the night. It was such fun. Before they went to sleep, they reminisced about the evening and how they were treated in this house. They liked how grown up they felt. Peter said, "I know we are in a different continent but it is hard for me to comprehend the difference in the kinds of fish and animals we see here." Andy responded with," I have been in the pet store at home and have seen a few of the fish they have for sale but it is nothing compared to what Mannie has here. The fish here are so bright colored. I am used to Buddy, our dog. Think of what it would be like to have Zoey for a pet."

Chapter 8

REVELATION OF THE GIFT FROM THE ALIENS.

When they woke up, they went to the kitchen to find Cama had fixed them breakfast on the patio. Afterwards, Mannie was going to show them what was in the rest of the yard.

"First", Mannie said, "Boys, this is a good time to talk about what happened when we were taken hostage. You can share whatever you're comfortable with as it will remain with me." Peter and Andy were silent for awhile then Peter began to tell him about what happened last year.

He told Mannie about getting lost, the fire, the cave, the bats, and the search for food and water. One thing he did not hold back on was how guilty he felt for not being responsible and betraying the trust his dad had in him. Andy chimed in by telling about the place they found that was so beautiful with waterfalls, abundant fish, and even a frog. He related about how they encountered two aliens. They were frightful looking at first until they realized that was how aliens really looked. The aliens could read the boys' minds.

Peter told how they used morse code with a flashlight to communicate. The aliens were stranded in the mountain like themselves. Their space ship was lodged inside and they needed the boys' help to free it. Before they exited the mountain, the aliens, who were superior intelligent beings, transmitted an energy to them. They felt stronger and smarter. Andy and Peter explained that they had no idea what the potential was.

They told Mannie that they stared into the eyes of the bandits who became mesmerized and changed their behavior.

Mannie listened carefully to the whole story, thanked them for sharing it with him, and most of all for being honest. He said, "I want you to know that you saved our lives and probably those of the airport staff.

Now no more feeling guilty about what you did last year. It would be a good idea to share this with your dad. He can help you with channeling this gift you received." He had one piece of advice for them to be careful to only use their powers for good. It was astounding to Peter and Andy that the Gift from the Aliens was acknowledged to be so positive to Mannie.

Peter thanked Mannie for giving them the chance to speak about it. Andy also added that he felt inspired by what he had said to them. Mannie just nodded saying, "Now outside we go. I am going to introduce you to the menagerie. There are some interesting specimens for you two to see. The Amazon Rain Forest hosts more than one-third of all species. Many of the species you will see here are on the endangered species list and I take this responsibility seriously. I do more than just house them. They are studied by specialists and environmentalists."

He took them to see some rare birds from the Amazon Basin. The first was the rare Spix Macaw that has a dark blue head, blue body, greenish belly, black mask and yellow eyes. They are rare due to the loss of natural habitat from deforestation and over collection of them. He then explained how many people bring him these types of birds and wildlife to preserve them in this sanctuary. He also had several types of parrots, toucans, and some scarlet macaws. When I am not here, Raol feeds and tends them. He told them of the varied birds that use the jungle for their home. Mannie added." I am not sure about how many species migrate from your country to South America. I believe the Bob-o-link, the Tundra Swan and some Sand Hill Cranes winter as far south as Argentina. That would make a good research project for either of you."

Another area had some reptiles which he named. There was the Anole lizard, yellow footed tortoise, numerous types of frogs, a crocodile, a large boa constrictor, and an anaconda snake. He told them that the Anaconda snake is a good swimmer, lives in the trees, and eats every week or so. It can be found in the shallow waters. The Amazon River has many sorts of crab, turtles, even dolphins and manatees. The dolphin is a river mammal that grows up to eight feet in length. It's color changes as it ages. Here is a bit of lore, the dolphin supposedly turns into a man and seduces

maidens by the river side. He chuckled as he said, "It is the opposite of the mermaid story." The manatee is both a mammal and herbivore. It is on the conservation list to be protected. He went on to tell stories about eels, sting rays, and fish species. Next he took them to see the largest rodent in the Amazon called capybara that looked like a guinea pig. As they walked past another cage, they heard deep, throated growling. As they approached the animal, it shrank back. Mannie told them that it was a black jaguar. Now he wondered to himself if the jaguar sensed the gift that the boys had but said nothing about it. He told them that the big cat is also on the endangered species list. The jaguar is a graceful animal that needs protection and is nearly extinct here in South America. The boys peered into the enclosure to see a sleek, black cat with piercing blue eyes like none they had ever seen before.

The boys were in a sort of daze after walking from one enclosure to another. Finally, Andy spoke up, "Mannie, I will never forget what we saw here today. Each animal has its own place that seems like it would have in it's natural environment." Then Peter added a comment that it was all clean with each animal content within it's enclosure. With this, Mannie beamed with pleasure.

It was getting quite hot as they turned to go back to the hacienda for lunch. While they were eating, Mannie said, "I heard you talking about getting some souvenirs for your family back home. Let me treat you to these. I have a friend who will bring a selection to the house and you can choose some.

He can package and mail them to your home. Would you be agreeable to this?" Peter answered that it would be just fine.

It was so exciting choosing some jewelry for their mom, sister and cousin. They wondered what to pick for Nate when they saw the perfect item. It was a miniature rickshaw called the moto-carro used as a taxi in Iquitos. For their grandparents, they choose some statues. They knew their dad would like to have a souvenir also so they chose a money clip for him. The vendor guaranteed Mannie that he would carefully wrap them and send them off tomorrow.

They sat in the shade for awhile then heard their dad approaching. He slapped the valise saying, "The deal is done! The plan completed, signed, sealed, and now I ready to deliver it to my company."

Mannie said, "Ok, then tomorrow at dawn, we board the 'Domitila' and head back. It is too late in the day to go now. We will have a pleasant evening here and get a good night's rest. I have some other cargo that I have to deliver plus some on the return trip so this is timely."

As they sat around that evening, he told them more stories about how the Andes Mountains, the longest range in the world, were formed more than 70 million years ago through tectonic forces thrusting up the mountains.

He told them stories of the mythical El Dorado. The stories were so delightful and they would always remember it.

Chapter 9

SABOTAGE OF AIRPLANE SUSPECTED

The alarm was set for 4:00 in the morning to prepare for the trip back to the United States. Brad arose to see Mannie leaving with Raol to the airport. Mannie said, "I received a call from the airport authorities about a disturbance in the hangar where my plane is stored. It appears there was a break-in. I am on the way over there now. Let the boys sleep in until I check this out. A close friend has alerted me that the drug cartel that held us hostage wants revenge for what happened. This may be retribution and I am worried that they damaged the airplane."

Raol returned shortly saying that Mannie instructed him to keep a close watch on the family. They were to stay in the hacienda and not go outside for now. He would call with updates.

Several hours later Peter and Andy arose alarmed that they had over slept wondering why their dad had not called for them. They were all packed ready to go. As they walked to the kitchen, the aroma of food was wafting down the hallway.

They knew that Cama was cooking up a storm. Yesterday she told them that it was so good to have someone to eat the food like the young boys did.

Their dad was in the kitchen having a cup of coffee. He looked up as the boys entered telling them to have a good meal then he would let them know what was happening. Peter said, "Dad, we were going to be leaving at dawn. You didn't awaken us. We want to know if something happened over night. Where is Mannie?"

Brad assured them that Mannie was just fine. After breakfast, he would fill them in on the details. Raol was in the kitchen as well but he didn't appear to be his smiley self. There was a sense of heaviness that the boys detected. They were happy to see Cama smiling as she served them a special breakfast.

Raol's phone chirped just as Peter and Andy finished eating. They noticed a shadow pass across his face as he shook his head. He passed the phone to Brad who spoke to Mannie. After that he looked to Peter and Andy saying, "There was a break-in at the hangar where the plane is stored. The authorities believe it was the drug cartel that held us hostage. Mannie had reported it to the government officials when we landed in Iquitos. The airport security know that there are bribes within the officials. One guard reported over-hearing them threaten to damage the plane. Mannie and the mechanic are doing a thorough inspection. It will take several hours though. I am going to call your mom and update her on the delay without alarming her."

Several hours later, Mannie called to say all appeared to be clear. He told Raol to bring Brad and the boys to the airport. Cama packed a basket of food that would last them for awhile. She took each boy and hugged him to her chest. She said, "Come back again. Be safe." She waved as Raol drove the jeep out of the compound to the airport where Mannie was waiting.

Brad held on to his valise and walked into the hangar to speak with Mannie before the boys and Raol came in. Mannie reported that he and the mechanic checked the oil lines and pressure gauges. The guard's presence must have alerted them before they could do damage. Most of the time, they put small pricks in the oil line. Then with the slow leak, the engine heats up. I feel confident that we will be safe but I have changed my flight plan just in case. He grabbed a sandwich from the food basket that Raol was bringing in as he climbed into the cock pit.

With a worried look at the boys, Mannie told Brad that bandits of this sort do not like to lose as it affects their status.

With this he called, "All aboard and off we go. Raol, please keep a close watch on the animal cages. They might think to let some of them loose or feed them poison. You and Cama stay close by. The authorities are on alert as well."

As the plane began its ascent, the sight below was phenomenal with the Amazon River basin in full view. Mannie said, "It fills me with awe each time I see this. Some people have called it 'empty land'. In a way, it is true. When you look at the canopy of trees making up the rain forest, the jungle area could solve the food problem of the world. The vast area has soil that is nutritionally poor. The dense forest is kept alive by the sun, the heavy rainfall, and the compost of leaves. Many of the deforested areas are now abandoned as no basic food crops will grow there. In the mountainous areas, it is a different story."

By now the airplane had leveled off flying a east-north-easterly direction according to the compass. The passengers settled back to enjoy the scenery and Mannie's stories. It would be at least four hours before they would stop again.

Mannie turned the plane to correct a slight flaw in the direction. As he did so, a plume of powder sprayed out of the control stick flying directly into his eyes. He screamed then slumped over the steering column causing it to jam heading them straight to the earth! As the plane nose dived, Brad reached over to shake Mannie with no luck. He tried to pull the steering stick up only to find that it was locked into position. They were headed for a crash into the dense forest below. He turned to look at his sons with a tenderness saying, "We are going to crash. I love you both but we will survive. Buckle tight and put your heads between your knees."

The noise was so loud with the engine whining at full speed. Brad looked at the gauges that were all going whacko. The plane was shaking and convoluting itself, spinning out of control. The pressure on the passenger's ears was tremendous with the rapid descent. The whole interior was filling with the white powder that made breathing quite difficult. Brad tried to open a side window finding it glued shut. It was sabotage for sure. While he tried to appear calm for the sake of his sons, he was reaching panic in his thoughts. He had to control these wild thoughts.

He reached for the Mic. on the Hallicrafter, saying "May Day! May day! Stinson plane filled with white powder. Pilot gone. Help us."

Chapter 10

AIRPLANE CRASHES IN THE JUNGLE

As the plane gyrated in its rapid descent, the sound of the engine now running at full throttle was deafening. It hit the treetops shaving off some branches with loud, booming noises. It jammed into the huge trees with the propellor partially sticking into the earth. The rest of the plane hung there then settled down farther into the forest. There was total silence for awhile with no movement in the airplane or in the forest.

Soon the forest resumed the usual noises with the curious monkeys swinging through the trees to investigate. They climbed into the plane chattering as they investigated what this was. As most animals, they were looking for food. One climbed up on Peter's shoulder and shook him awake. He looked around to orient himself. He could not believe the mess around him. He reached over to shake Andy. He called his name as well. To his relief, Andy stirred trying to jump then realized he was belted into his seat. He looked over at Peter and asked him if he was okay. They both felt their feet, hands and heads. Then knowing they were alright, they unbelted with Peter climbing into the front seul to check on their dad. There was no movement. Blood was running down his dad's face. Peter called out to him. With no response, he felt his dad's wrist getting a pulse. With relief, he told Andy that Dad was alive. Then applying what he had learned in first aid class, he gently shook him plus calling out to him. "Dad," he called. There was no response so he took off the seat belt and pressed his ear to his dad's chest. There was a strong heart beat which gave him hope. Andy said, "Maybe Dad is in a coma."

Peter shook his head then asked Andy to give him a tee shirt from his pack. He gently wiped the blood from his dad's face.

Andy leaned over Mannie to call him. When he did not answer, Peter turned around to him to check for a pulse. He couldn't detect any thus assuming that Mannie was killed in the crash.

The jungle began its encroachment. The monkeys had crawled out but the giant ants were already climbing up the side of the plane. Both Andy and Peter began assessing their situation. The instruments appeared to be either smashed or hanging loose. Andy reached out and took the compass out of the dashboard. It was useable so he put it in his back pack. He told Peter that the two way communications radio looked broken.

After looking at his dad's cell phone, Peter discovered it didn't work. He reached over to get Mannie's. Never had he been so close to someone he believed was dead. He shook his head, gritted his teeth and reached into Mannie's shirt pocket. This phone didn't work either. What would they do with no means to call for help? Peter remembered that his dad had called 'May Day' on the Hallicrafter. Surely the control tower at Iquitos would have been monitoring the frequency. He was going to count on that so they would know what happened.

Then he remembered there was a "ham radio" by Mannie's leg and perhaps that was still useable. He crawled out of the airplane to get to the door by the pilot seat from the outside. It was almost impossible to reach as the plane was not entirely on the ground. Reaching for a handle, he managed to pull himself up without toppling the entire plane over. Then he jumped on the wing to access the door opening it enough to reach in for the Mic. He compressed it and heard a squelch! That was a good sound to him. He called out for anyone listening, "My name is Peter. Our plane crashed in the rain forest north east of Iquitos, Peru. The pilot was killed. My father is badly hurt and appears to be in a coma. Call the airport in Iquitos as they knew our route. Help! Help! We can not go back up the river. We are lost here in this jungle. Again help us." Andy told Peter that he was grateful that Mannie had told them about the emergency situation and what to say on the "ham radio." Peter agreed.

With that mission accomplished, Peter approached Andy to put together a plan. "Andy, this is worse than where we were last year. We must look ahead to get our dad to a doctor for help. I believe we will need to test our 'Gift from the Aliens' to the utmost in order to survive. First let's see what we have and what we can use from the airplane." Andy agreed and took a deep breath. Fate handed them an almost impossible situation. They would face this together as they needed to save their dad! They looked at each other and made a pact as they thought of their mom and the family.

They looked in their packs for what they could use. The one thing they did have was bright flashlights but there was not much else right now. The food that Cama had sent with them would be divvied out as needed. With this heat, it would spoil quickly. Peter and Andy wished for some of the venison jerky that had saved them last year. While it was so hot and humid, it would only get worse. Mannie had told them about how the mosquitoes and bugs swarm to surround the human body. It would take a great deal of insecticide to protect them from the insistent barrage from them.

The two brothers looked around at this primeval forest. All they could see were rope-like vines everywhere among the thick undergrowth. There were thorny bushes and gray-green trees covered with moss. The ferns were tall, feathery plants. The noise was incessant with the chattering and squawking from all sorts of animals. It was un-nerving to Peter and Andy as they looked up and all they could see was the canopy of tree tops with small rays of sunshine beaming through. They had no idea where they were. In desolation, Peter said, "Andy, we are lost in this rain forest jungle and no one knows where to look for us."

One thing Peter wished they had was a machete. They needed to cut thick branches and trees that were blocking most of the sunlight so they could be seen from above in case someone heard them call for help. From down here, it was a whole different scene.

They looked the plane over carefully making the decision that although Mannie was no longer alive, they would have to stay inside for the night to keep the bugs off themselves. They also knew there were vampire bats and huge snakes. With this decision made, they took a tarp and covered Mannie with it. A great sadness came over them as they looked at him. He was a friend they treasured. They lowered the back of their dad's seat. They decided to leave him where he was for now but put a piece of light cloth over him to protect him from the incessant attack by flying insects.

Then they set to work to plan what to do next. They surveyed the portion of the plane that had the two passengers seats and decided to take them out. Peter suggested they build a raft and float the river to the next settlement. Andy had some good ideas about using the panels in the passenger section. There were some tie downs that would come in handy also. They gave each other a high five and set to work to save their dad and themselves. The bugs were already becoming thick.

In the cargo area, they found some insecticide but decided to hold off using it for now. They found a first aid kit and a machete in a tool kit that Peter had thought would come in handy. The first job was to get the material ready for building a raft that they needed ready by tomorrow.

They began to toss out the pieces as they removed them. Andy thought the raft should be six feet wide and longer if they could locate some trees. When the plane was cleaned out, they put the seats back against the wall and that would be their tent for the night.

The boys found a parachute which they could use for water proofing and lots of string that would help in tying the logs together. They began to tire and sat down in the compartment to eat. Cama had sent some fresh fruit which they ate first saving the sandwiches for later on. She had sent some juice containers but not much water. After they had eaten, a new idea came to them to cover the plane with the parachute to further protect them from the wildlife and the insects.

With that done, they packed themselves inside the plane and took a nap. The jungle noise persisted. Andy lay there thinking he imagined the night to be quiet. He reached out for Peter who crawled close to him. It would be a long night with neither of them getting much sleep. The jungle noise continued.

At the break of dawn, they crawled out of the plane and lifted the side of the parachute to survey the area. They agreed to do some work before they would eat any food.

Peter searched through the side tool compartment for string, line, or objects like a saw. He was grateful to have found the machete but that wasn't enough. Digging deeper, he found some plastic food packets. He quickly called Andy, "Look, here is some dried food. Just what we need."

Peter left Andy to sort through the wood pieces and began to walk in a circle around the area to look for some logs. He knew they would have to be light enough to float. They could mount the wood pieces on top for a deck. After several times around, he expanded the area but stayed close within view of the plane and Andy." Finally", he shouted, "Andy, come here and see if these will work." As Andy inspected them he agreed that they looked to be a possibility.

The brothers dragged the logs into the area then built a fire to help dry the work area. There was plenty of underbrush.

Peter went to check on their dad and saw that his condition remained the same. The food basket was the next operation as hunger set in. Now feeling better, the job to scrape the logs was begun. A pattern was laid out. Andy seemed to know how to organize them so Peter continued with the prep work. The machete and his Swiss Army knife were working well. It took them most of the morning to complete enough logs to ready the binding.

With both of the boys cutting the binding from the parachute, it didn't take too long. They found some wire in their packs then searched for some vines they thought would tie well. Soon the logs were ready for the wood paneling which both wondered how to secure it. An idea came to Andy. He suggested they tap a tree for the sap, burn it, and cool the material just like the ancient Indians did. This would water proof the paneling.

It would take more hours that they were ready to sacrifice for a more secure deck. Andy took on the challenge to do this. Peter looked over the airplane again thinking he could dismantle the propellor to use as an oar. Using great caution, he feared any movement would shift the angle of the plane. While they worked, the boys talked to each other sharing ideas and remembering some of the things that Mannie had told them about the jungle, the river, and the Indians that have lived there for generations.

Peter remembered the story Mannie had told about the quinine as a healing agent that took him in search of the tree from which to cut the bark. Who knew what else they would need and what faced them with the river creatures! They joked as they said that it would be their good fortune if a large llama would stroll through to help them haul the raft to the river! Andy said, "No such luck for us. We will need to move it with logs."

As the day progressed, the raft was nearly finished. They decided that they should move it closer to the river in readiness for tomorrow. They could talk about how to operate it with the long night hours ahead of them. The bugs were huge and bit hard leaving blood tracks even though they sprayed themselves. The net they had spread over their dad was black with the bugs that were attracted to the human scent.

They put together an idea on how to move their dad from the plane to the raft which was now secured close to the trees along the river.

Then Andy remembered the trapeze he had built for Peter last year. They could use the parachute and some foliage between some tree trunks and pull it to the raft.

Andy and Peter were anxious to get going but steeled themselves to be patient. They remembered the aliens in their space ship and how they had to stay to find a source of food. That lesson now served them well.

They bunked down for the night but sleep was slow to come. Andy spoke aloud about the dangers they could face. He talked about the stories Raol and Mannie had told them about how the foreigners from Europe attempted to civilize this part of the country. Many of them traveled upstream from the area where the Amazon met the Atlantic Ocean and were never heard of again. He told Peter, "I am afraid that could happen to us also. The rain forest would swallow us up." They discussed the possibility that if they stayed here that perhaps their chances of rescue would be better as they hoped someone heard their distress call. Finally, Peter mused aloud that he had heard that there is a signal that airplanes send out when they crash but neither of them knew how to check this or if that was smashed also. They agreed that it was a better choice to continue with the raft and go down stream.

They finally fell asleep and slept most of the night. Upon awakening from their second night in the airplane, they checked on their dad. The realization that their dad did not make any sound confirmed for them what they had suspected. He probably had received a concussion causing the coma. They would have to be very careful when they moved him so as not to incur more damage. Andy bent down and kissed his dad's cheek vowing to be strong for him, "Peter and I will get you to a place where there are people who will help you."

Chapter 11

RAFT ON THE AMAZON

They were ready to secure the tools, food basket, and supplies to the raft. The operation of moving Dad would be next. Andy asked what were they going to do to ensure that the valise did not get wet. Andy said, "There are important papers in it and we have to find a sealing bag somewhere in this plane. That is our future and we need to keep it safe." So they searched.

In the meantime in the outside world, the news spread fast. There were two boys lost in the remote jungles of the Rain Forest along the Amazon River Basin in South America. The 'May Day' call was acknowledged and the authorities were sending out search parties. Then a 'ham operator' in Colombia heard the message from Peter. This also was spread across the bands. All forms of social media spread the message about the young boys.

The bad news was that the drug cartel also heard that the passengers had survived. They wanted them dead and began their own search to complete their mission. Raol also heard this and decided to call the authorities he could trust to stop the bandits. The news that the pilot did not survive the crash saddened him. What would become of himself and Cama? He would worry about that later as the protection of the boys was more important.

Raol wondered if the bandits would use speed boats to search for the boys. He fretted about being powerless and could only imagine what the youngsters and their dad were encountering in the jungle. If only he had access to a boat and could go to find them. Then he remembered the last instructions that Mannie had issued before leaving that he was to protect the house and the compound.

When the mail man came to the boys' home that day, he delivered a package from Peru that contained the precious items picked out by Peter and Andy. Their mom broke down in tears. She wondered where they were and what condition they were in. The radio spread the news that the father was injured and she wondered how badly. She carefully opened the package taking out each item and laying them on the table. Touching each item with wonder of how her sons had so carefully chosen items specially suited for each of the family. She held the money clip for her husband close to her heart. A strong sense of peace overcame her as it seemed she had just received a message assuring her that they would all be fine. This prompted her to call the family together to give comfort to each other.

Abby shed some tears hugging her mom and Nate. Allie, her parents, and the grandparents came to spend the night to await news. They were amazed at the gifts for them. Nate sat down to play with the miniature rickshaw. Allie and Abby admired their jewelry. Grandpa and Grandma treasured the Incan statues that would sit next to the black ebony statues from Africa in their book shelves.

Peter and Andy oblivious to all this continued their project to keep the valise protected. They found a canvas bag and strapped it to the seat. This caused some elation for them. They sat down to eat lunch before moving their dad and getting the raft onto the river. The boys recalled some things that Mannie had told them. The river rises and falls quickly so be aware to watch for floating leaves, logs, and bits of foam all hurrying to the Atlantic Ocean. He had talked of the channels that had no outlets. It would be easy to get trapped in there.

It was almost as if he was there, telling them to watch the ripples caused by the wind fighting the current running fast in the Amazon. He told them stories of how people lost their lives by not paying attention on choosing sloping banks rather than between steep ones. The boys decided that one of the brothers would probe the water in the front end of the raft while the other brother used the steering log at the back.

They appreciated the ability to think clearly using the gift of logic from the aliens. Now the effort began to move their dad via the trapeze. They were careful not to cause any sudden movements. It wasn't easy but finally they had him on the raft. Andy went back for the seat that he then secured to the decking.

They had made a covering for this portion of the deck out of some palms to protect their dad from the glaring sun.

For themselves, they wove palms into a hat and tied them on with vines. Peter did one final walk about to ensure that they took any or all items that they possibly could use. A thought struck Peter that they should take the cushions from the airplane to use in case the raft shifted causing one of them to fall off. He called to Andy to help him attach them to the back packs. Andy suggested using the vines for that and to hook themselves to the raft for balance. All this took time but both of them knew it would be life saving as they traversed the Amazon River. They didn't talk about what would happen if one of them accidently fell into the river. All precautions needed to be taken to prevent this.

Finally Peter said, "I think we are ready to tackle the Amazon River and find a doctor for dad." They strapped their back packs on and used the insect spray. The insects were a constant irritation. They were careful with the parachute as that would protect them at night. It would be used as protection from the flying insects and the vampire bats that puncture the skin then secrete a substance that prevents clotting as Mannie had told them. They shoved off the bank onto the river but left a marker on trees so the plane could be found. The day was very hot with little wind. Peter worried that his dad would get dehydrated so he stooped to wet his lips. He didn't want to drip anything down his throat as he may choke.

Several hours later, the brothers changed places with Peter taking the probing. The going was slow, but it was better this way. The boys took turns eating a bit and drinking fluids to keep themselves hydrated also. After many hours of steering the raft, they looked for a place to dock. The greatest concern would be to find a stable water level.

They took turns concentrating on the shoreline until finally it appeared. Now they could dock the raft and unload their dad.

They decided to pull the raft out of the river and put the parachute over it like a tent. While it was hard work, the effort was worth it when the bugs came in thick droves. It looked like a black cloud.

Tonight they would need to keep a fire burning to scare away the snakes and wildlife. It would be another long night for them. Peter asked Andy about taking turns sleeping to guard the raft. After awhile, Andy agreed as there were Indian tribes nearby who possibly could surround them.

They had no inkling that the bandits were searching the river for them until Andy heard a boat and crept out to the shoreline to observe. He was amazed at the depth of his vision and looked up into the sky whispering a thanks to the aliens. The boat appeared to be sleek with high speeds. Guns were mounted on the deck. The driver of the boat peered to the shoreline with binoculars. There were four men who looked to be some mean hombres.

Quietly with great agility, Andy sped back to where their dad and Peter were. He shook Peter quickly saying, "Ssh, There are some people out on the river in a speed boat. They look mean, Peter." Andy added, "I wonder if they belong to the bandits? It couldn't be any search and rescue to aid us. Come with me quickly. You can not believe how clear I can see and I am wondering if your sight will be the same." They crept to the shoreline lying as low as possible. The insects were ferocious but they had to endure that. Peter looked up and down the river to verify the description that Andy had given him. There it was!

He poked Andy and whispered that they should return to put out the fire as the smoke possibly could be seen even though they were hidden from view. They needed to protect not only their dad but also themselves. Back at the campsite, they could speak louder to make new plans since this danger had surfaced.

Peter told Andy to lie down under the parachute to get some shut eye as he would watch the area. Peter concentrated with all his might to keep his hearing as keen as possible. This also helped to keep him awake. He could hear the insects and the night creatures that were so loud to him that it almost hurt his ears. He stayed in this position until dawn. Upon waking Andy, they talked of alternative options. They ate the last sandwiches from the basket.

Peter told Andy that he was going to start a small fire to heat water in his Boy Scout kettle to mix with the Quinine he had collected. He hoped that it may be a remedy to help their dad.

He asked Andy to go closer to the shore and keep up the vigil. Peter slowly rubbed the Quinine bark around inside his dad's mouth very carefully not to cause any choking. There was still no response from his dad. He carefully changed the bandage to the injured area on his dad's head noticing that there was no more bleeding. He bathed the area with the warm water then put some iodine from the first aid kit on the area before he put a new bandage on. He whispered into his dad's ear, "Dad, please get well. We all need you. I love you."

As he was doing this, an idea popped into his head. He went in search of Andy who reported there was no activity. It would be safe to start putting the raft into the river and resume the float. Peter talked to Andy about his idea. He said, "We should look for an Indian settlement and ask for help. Remember Mannie telling us stories about how they have remedies that work. What do you think?" Andy agreed and added that the Natives could give them some protection from the bandits. With the plan in place now, they rolled the raft into the water slowly as not to jar their comatose father. Andy took a last look at the place where the raft had been secured catching his breath as he saw a huge Anaconda snake sliding around. Here in the jungle, an Anaconda Snake could be fatal to them. It was frightening to imagine what would have happened had they not left when they did.

Andy took the front end for probing with Peter in the rear. They set for the fast stream in the river. They had a new mission that they knew would give them the chance to save their dad and themselves.

Chapter 12

ARRIVE AT INDIAN SETTLEMENT

The rhythm that they had devised was working quite well. As they floated the river, Andy kept an eye on his dad. He looked back at his brother, smiling. Peter smiled back to give him more confidence. Their relationship had changed so much. It was as if they were equal to each other and trusted the knowledge each could impart.

Today the river was showing its fury with the wind whipping up the waves making steering nearly impossible. They both had to exert all their force to keep it steady. The water splashed onto the deck and hit the seat they had secured their dad on. With the hot sun beating down on them, Peter wondered how long they could endure this struggle. They had virtually no shade and were sweating like pigs. Peter and Andy could not change places either as they had to hang on to the steering poles.

It would have been so easy just to quit and let the raft go on its own. Peter wondered how long Andy could keep his position in probing. He began to feel sorry for himself and resentful that they were here on this massive river. It seemed to want only to swamp them so they would drown.

He and Andy exchanged a look of futility. How were they to continue?

They couldn't hear each other above the roar of the wind and the waves.

Andy kept looking around to see if the bandits were following them.

Believing that they would get shot ending their lives provided the motivation to continue. The hours passed when Andy pulled the compass out of his pocket to see what direction they were going. It revealed that they had changed from northeast to more east. They had studied the maps from the airplane and those from the airport book shop where they had purchased them that seemed an eternity ago.

This jived with the maps. He motioned to Peter that they would need to steer more to the northeast to get to the other side of the river. Peter gave him a questioning look but motioned alright. He would accept what Andy was motioning for him to do.

Peter looked over the side of the raft and spotted a huge crocodile. He checked his dad's arm to make sure it was secure. The crocodile's eyes and nose protruded out of the water. Peter motioned to Andy to be careful as he feared the crocodile could upend the raft. He remembered Mannie telling him that some of the crocodiles in the Amazon grow to more than 50' in length. As it glided along-side, Peter stared at it as long as he could. Finally it slid away down deep into the muddy water. What a relief!

It took them several more hours with extreme concentration to execute the move. They slid the raft to the shoreline into a small bay. Andy jumped out to secure the line nearly falling into the water. He ached so much he could hardly get his legs and arms to do anything more. Peter got out the quinine bark wetting it to swirl in his dad's mouth. He almost tripped which would have caused him to lose the bark. He gritted his teeth and willed his body to move. His dad did not move at all. Peter was afraid that they were losing him. He swirled the wet bark in his dad's mouth along with dabbing some cool water on his forehead.

He jumped to the shore and hugged Andy saying, "It looked like we had bit the bullet today. You saved us you know. Now let's eat before we pull the raft up to the shore. I am thankful to be out of the main stream. Dad hasn't changed and I am getting worried, Andy."

They both needed rest but couldn't take the time. The red welts from the biting insects were numerous causing severe itching and burning. The brothers hurried as fast as they could.

Finally the raft was secured and their dad was in the shade covered with the parachute in a tent-like position. They lay down on the deck of the raft to catch their breath. They sat up as they knew they were not alone. They were surrounded by many Indian people painted in red color, wearing hats woven from palm leaves.

The Indians grunted pushing at the boys to stand up. The right hand gesture of good will was ignored. They forced the boys to turn each way and around. The language they used was unfamiliar to Peter and Andy who thought that the natives would have adopted some Spanish words. One of them reached over to look under the parachute tent then jumped back when he saw a human body under it. This forced Peter to grunt also. He motioned upward with his right hand then pointed to Andy and himself to signify the dad and sons. One of them seemed to comprehend so Peter continued. He put his arms out like wings on an airplane making the droning sound brought it swiftly down to simulate the crash. He pointed to the injury on his father's head and closed his eyes. He then shook his own head to indicate that his father is in a coma not dead.

This seemed to be working so he continued to point to his father and the Indians running his finger to his dad and the Indians to ask for help.

The Indians stepped back with some of them leaving. Andy asked Peter, "What do think of them leaving?" Peter answered with a remembrance of a story that Mannie had told them about how the explorers came bringing diseases with them that wiped out the Indians by the thousands. He said, "I felt a connection with one of the elders. I would bet they are holding a conference of whether to let us enter or ship us out?" Andy agreed commenting that it was a good assumption on Peter's part. He marveled at how Peter had communicated with them asking for their help. Andy said, "At first I was frightened by the red color as to me that represents conflict and danger. I didn't get that sense here, did you?"

Just then the Indians returned with an Indian Elder who had no paint on his face. He looked into the eyes of the boys then somewhat startled, he turned away. He walked over to the raft leaning over Brad and lifted one of his eye lids. He turned the head some to each side inspecting the neck area. He ran his hands over the entire body very slowly humming some tune the whole while. He moved to the center of the body, closed his eyes, moving his hands, and stood that way like he was a statue.

He turned to look at the tribesmen then motioned for them to carry Brad on a mat of woven palm leaves. They lifted him carefully following the Elder to the village. Peter and Andy remained behind waiting for an invitation that did not come. So they sat on the raft resting and getting restored after the turmoil of the Amazon River that day. Both of them believed they had accomplished their purpose which was to get their dad to a doctor. The old Indian man was going to heal their dad for which they were grateful. Because the raft wasn't visible from the main stream, they felt safe to crawl under the parachute tent to get some sleep.

What seemed like hours later, several Indian men came to escort them to the village. Peter wanted to tell them about the bandits that were searching for them but didn't know how to gesture it. He told Andy that he was going to let fate handle the bandits. These people have survived here for hundreds of years and would know what bandits can do. They will be able to cope with what comes along.

The escorts took them to a small hut that was made of thatched palms that circled a courtyard. There were not many visible occupants and the boys wondered if they stayed hidden until a judgment could be made. Peter brought his dad's valise, the food basket, and his back pack. Andy brought the tool kit and his backpack. They invited the Indian who was probably their guard to look inside so he would see they had no weapons. Andy handed the machete to the guard and bowed.

They entered the hut that was pleasantly comfortable with no insects, bugs, or spiders. Andy thought this was a good deal. He was hungry and dug into the basket to get some food out. No one came to look in on them.

The boys took turns sleeping just in case they were called to the central hut.

The next morning they looked out to see what was going on. Activity had resumed in the village that made the boys feel they were accepted.

All day they waited with no word or sign of any kind. Finally Peter said, "This must be a good sign that they are making progress with Dad. I am certain they would have come to get us if his condition changed." Andy was getting restless though. He wanted to move around but Peter cautioned to use patience. They spoke about what their mom and family were experiencing after hearing this news. Andy said, 'Not only our family but also the family of Mannie will suffer. It will a loss for Raol and Cama. We had so much to deal with after the crash that now I can feel emotion.

I wonder if Mom received our package with the souvenirs we sent them. Somehow that package may help her to bear the burden of wondering if we are alright."

Chapter 13

DRUG BANDITS CAPTURED BY INDIANS

It had been a long night of waiting. With morning, there was still no news. Several hours later, Andy peered out between the slats to see what the commotion was. All he could see were the bandits surrounded by the Indians. The hands of the bandits were bound with vines. The Indians were carrying the bandit's weapons. He almost shouted out then restrained himself. Now he knew why they were kept secluded. The Indians knew all about this. Peter crawled over to watch.

He did not know what their customs were but figured it would not go well for the bandits. He saw an Indian put a conch shell to his mouth and blow it. Suddenly a crowd of Indians all painted in red appeared.

Peter and Andy watched in amazement and wonder as they pushed the drug bandits into the center of the ring. As one of the Elder Indians lifted a long pipe to his lips, he blew hard. A dart flew out of the pipe hitting the first bandit. This was repeated until the four of them were all hit.

Within a matter of seconds, they dropped dead and were carried off into the forest. No one knew that the boys had watched this whole ceremony. Peter and Andy fell back on their sleeping mats laughing with relief that the danger in their lives was now gone. They could relax and wait to hear about the healing of their dad. They knew everything was going to be fine.

The next morning, the guard who was stationed by the hut opened the straw latch motioning for the boys to come out and follow him. They were taken to a large hut that appeared to be a meeting room where there were many Indians seated in a circle on the ground. One chief stood up and motioned for the boys to come sit by him. He spoke broken English and asked their names. Andy looked at Peter and nodded his head so Peter spoke for them. The chief asked where they were from and how they got to the village. So Peter told him in a slow way. Occasionally, the chief looked to the crowd and spoke. Peter told them about the business trip, the bandits, Mannie, and the airplane crash. He told them that Mannie had no pulse and their dad had a concussion. So they built the raft to go down the river looking for a doctor. Then followed by the bandits, they had to take great care not to be seen by the speed boat. The chief listened and told them that Mannie was alive. The powder he breathed in put him in a hibernation-like state. He was a descendant from this tribe but left it to go to Iquitos years ago. The chief knew about the story but wanted to hear it from the boys. He told them that while their dad was healing, it would take some time. The chief assured them that the bandits would no longer be a danger to them.

Andy asked if they could see their dad. The chief put up his hand denying the request. The healing ceremony is sacred. Your dad is being tended by our shaman who uses a variety of barks, leaves, resin, and seeds. The shaman are respected as being spiritual specialists who have access to the spiritual world which gives them the power to see into the future and experiences from far away.

He added that the boys were permitted to walk around the village. If they had questions they should motion to this hut then he would come to answer them. He explained that this is a tribe that did not include Spanish when the explorers came. Our language is Quechuan Inca. Peter said that he and Andy wanted to get cleaned up. The chief then put up a hand which led to one Indian leaving. He brought an older woman to the door who shook her head up and down. The boys thanked the chief then followed the Indian woman. She reminded them of Cama which made them smile.

She took them to her hut where there were other younger boys. She made gestures that the boys would take them to a bathing area and handed them some grass skirts to wear. It was a bright and warm day with the bathing pool filled with clear, blue water. The boys frolicked in it, splashing each other with much laughter. Andy was the first to make gestures which they seemed to understand. He told them that it was great to feel clean. Peter also shook his head to agree. They put on the skirts that were quite comfortable as they were woven from palm fibers.

At first, Andy held back some as he wondered about wearing a palm skirt made from the aguaji palm tree. He looked around to see them all looking at him so he put it on. Their clothes were gathered up to be cleaned.

Their hosts asked them to follow them taking them to their game area to challenge each other in sporty events. It was delightful for Peter and Andy to feel so welcomed to this secluded band of Indians. They were hungry and gestured to eat. Their new friends took them to their hut where there was food set out. The fruit was delicious.

The day passed quickly with the night's activities ahead of them piqued the curiosity of Peter and Andy. Though the younger boys of the tribe were not welcome in the big circle, they could sit at the fringes to watch the older men go through some dances. They almost fell asleep and asked to go to their hut. They talked and reviewed what they had learned about the Yagua tribe that day knowing they respected the long history of ancestors. They dropped onto the sleeping mats and fell asleep.

Chapter 14

FINAL DAYS AT THE SETTLEMENT

They heard a noise at the opening of their hut to see Mannie standing there. He was a welcome sight even though he looked haggard and worn. They jumped up giving him a big hug with tears in their eyes. Mannie choked up and coughed to cover up his emotion.

He brought news that their dad was awake and recovering. He would take them to him later after they exchanged information. First Peter said, "Mannie, we thought you died in the plane crash. We checked for a pulse and there didn't appear to be any. So we covered you with a tarp to keep the insects off you."

He chuckled saying, "You two saved my life again by doing that." He explained about the powder he had ingested, its effect on him, and the recovery period. The bandits had come to look around the plane but did not see him as he had the tarp covering him. As they left, he crawled out from under the tarp and saw them return to the boat. He fiddled with the radio and needed to put wires back together then called the control tower. By asking them not to broadcast his condition, he wanted to keep the news from the bandits. The tower notified Raol and Cama that he was going to be ok. Raol got a boat taking him home in order to recover.

He asked the boys to tell him step by step what they did from the time the plane crashed to now. He marveled as they laid out the project plans then finding the means to make it happen. They apologized for ripping the paneling out of 'Domitila'. He pushed his arm down scoffing at that.

They told about steering the raft by recalling what he had told them during one of his stories. He was silent as they walked through each day with him.

Mannie listened intently as they described how they built the raft, the water proofing process, and the quinine. At first, the forest was a scary and noisy place but they adapted as they knew they had to for survival and to get their dad to a doctor. They repeated the part about the snake and the crocodile but that wasn't the worst. It was the danger of the bandits searching for them along the river. He chuckled as they told him about the black cloud of insects and how they used the parachute to protect themselves from the insects.

He kept shaking his head in amazement. Finally he complimented them on using their gift to the optimum saying, "The Aliens would be as proud of you as I am. You saved us all. The bandits are gone as well." They shook their heads telling Mannie they saw what happened, relieved that the threat was gone. "It was most fortunate that you chanced upon this tribe of people, my people, who have been in this area for centuries.

They live mostly off the river and forest by hunting and fishing. Many of them are artisans with skills like making jewelry and animal carvings that the chief takes to Iquitos to sell during his shopping for supplies. In fact, the gifts that you chose for your family came from this tribe.

They are a caring people blessed with a wonderful shaman who has healed your Dad. I am proud to be a Yagua Indian. I used to paint myself with the red seeds from the Annatto plant. You mentioned the blow guns which our tribe still uses today to hunt for monkey, sloths and more.

The tubes are hand crafted with different lengths. Some quivers have piranha teeth which sharpen the darts. The lethal poison coats the tips made from boiling down a combination of roots and plants. It is fast acting causing paralysis and suffocation," he explained to them.

Andy told him that his grandmother had visited an art exhibit that told about the violence endured by the Peruvians some decades ago due to political struggles. She remembered the beautiful textiles woven with animals, birds, and snakes in the materials. I remember her saying that it was remarkable to see the beauty among the struggles. Mannie shook his head in understanding that it was a dark period. Though his tribe, due to its isolation, did not suffer like some others. "Now", he said, "it is time to see your dad."

As they entered the hut where he was, they saw how clean and neat the area was. Their Dad was lying in a hammock resting. They walked quietly not wanting to disturb him. He sensed their presence opening his eyes with great love shining through. "My boys," he said, "You saved my life again." They reached out to his open arms so grateful to see him alive and well again. They sat down by his side to be close to him. He asked them to tell their story. This time they included the encounter with the aliens last summer, the gift from them, then continued with rescuing themselves from the bandits. He told them that he had questions but couldn't fathom what he had just heard. With that he said, "So that was why your grades were so high on your reports. Now I understand and we will keep this between ourselves. You can come to me anytime to talk about it. It will be your choice. The aliens gave you a gift that enabled you two to save our lives as we had fatal encounters here in this beautiful country also holding danger and evil.

We learned so much about each other. Soon we will go home. I talked with your mom this morning to tell her that we will be going back on the airline in a day. I will be ready to travel according to my personal doctor, the Shaman. Your mom told me that they received a package from you two. You rascals, when did you do this? I'll bet Mannie had a hand in it."

Peter and Andy thought this was about the best day in their lives as they held their Dad's hand in theirs. They handed the valise to their dad with a smile. He was overcome with delight. The Rainforest, the jungle, and the mighty Amazon will remain in their minds and hearts for ever! They looked at each other needing no words.

Edwards Brothers Malloy
Thorofare, NJ USA
May 14, 2013